MIKE YOUN

SUPERTED
ON PLANET SPOT

Illustrations by Tony Hutchings

Muller

Deep in space there is a very unusual planet. It has nine moons, which is quite usual. Its atmosphere consists of thick, white clouds, which is quite usual. But on the clouds are green spots — that *is* unusual! This is the planet Spot.

Look! Here is a rocket ship made out of space junk. Square metal tiles are beginning to peel off its hull like pieces of worn carpet. As it comes out of a cloud, through the grimy, scratched window of the cockpit we can see the glassy staring eyes of three weird astronauts — Texas Pete, Bulk, and Skeleton. They are on their way to the planet Spot.

On the surface of the unusual planet, a teddy bear is talking to a Spot family. There is his friend Spottyman, Spottyman's mother Mrs Spot and sister Blotch. Spotty is holding a container of cosmic dust which he had mined on one of his recent space adventures. Cosmic dust is the magic ingredient that Spottyman used to bring SuperTed to life.

Spotty is worried. "Where can I hide the cosmic dust, Mum? It's very precious."

"Have you forgotten?" asks Mrs Spot in surprise. "It's perfectly safe, because there are no thieves on Spot. Put it on that shelf."

The planet is looming larger and larger on the video screen inside Tex's scrappy spacecraft. Bulk is at the controls; Tex is leaning on a wooden bunk. Skeleton is stretched out in a fancy, decorated coffin.

"Bulk! Put on the brakes, we're almost there!" shouts Tex. "We'll steal that cosmic dust of Spottyman's and rule the universe."

Bulk pulls at the lever, which comes away in his hand. He shows it to Tex. "Is this the brake, Tex?"

On the screen, the planet Spot seems to be hurtling towards them.

On a multi-coloured lawn, beside a fountain that gushes green bubbles, Spotty, SuperTed and Blotch are playing with a spotty ball.

In the distance, a dark object falls from the sky. It screams across the horizon and shoots over them, just missing the dome. CRASH! It plunges into a ravine some distance away.

"Galloping Gooseberries, Spotty! What was that?" cries SuperTed.

They dash to the edge of the ravine, where smoke can be seen curling into the sky. Ted whispers his secret, magic word and, in a flash, changes into SuperTed. Spottyman straps on his rocket pack. They fly off to investigate.

On the other side of the ravine, away from the smoking wreck of the spaceship, Texas Pete is looking like a battered cowboy who has just competed in a very tough rodeo. He crawls over the side of the ravine onto a ledge, where he finds two bones.

"Looks like Skeleton is a goner," he says, sadly. "Where's that Bulk?"

Meanwhile, SuperTed and Spotty are standing over a blackened hole in the ground. Smoke still curls upwards. Pieces of twisted metal are strewn on the ground. SuperTed is puzzled.

"It looks like a very old rocket ship from Earth. But whose is it?"

They look around, and SuperTed finds something. A slipper!

Near the Spotty home, Blotch is giggling and pointing. Sitting on the multi-coloured lawn, still dazed from his fall, is a fat man with no spots . . . Bulk.

"Who are you?" asks Blotch, politely. "What are you doing?"

"My name is Bulk. I've come to steal the cosmic dust."

"Oh really. I'll show you where it is." Blotch takes Bulk innocently by the hand and leads him towards the house.

All the time, Texas Pete has been watching them from a ledge above the house. He has overheard everything.

SuperTed and Spotty are standing by the wreck, looking worried. They guess that Texas Pete may be somewhere near.

"You stay and search the ravine, Spotty. I'll fly back to the dome in case Tex should find his way there," says SuperTed. Spotty agrees. SuperTed has made the right decision.

Bulk is walking out of the Spotty dome, carrying a jar of glowing cosmic dust. Blotch is with him. Tex is lurking behind the dome, ready to pounce.

Zoom . . . From out of the sky SuperTed flies and lands on the lawn. Texas Pete, faster than a rattler in the grass, pushes back Bulk and grabs hold of the child. "Don't come near me, you stupid little bear, or the kid might get hurt. Come on, Bulk. Bring the cosmic dust. We'll steal the Spotty rocket and plunder the universe! Ha Ha Ha!"

As Spottyman flies back over the ravine, he notices something on a ledge. "It's Skeleton's ribcage. It looks as if he's had it."

The Spotty rocket is parked beside the lawn on a ledge near the edge of the ravine. Tex and Bulk are walking backwards towards it. Tex is holding the child. As they near the ledge, Bulk slips clumsily, grabs Tex's leg, and pulls him over the ledge. Blotch and the jar of cosmic dust are sent flying.

The child falls head over heels down the ravine. Whoosh! SuperTed flies out of nowhere and plucks Blotch out of the air. The cosmic dust spills out of the jar and floats down the ravine like sparkling rain.

Some of the dust falls on Skeleton's ribcage . . . Falabalam! Skeleton regains his full shape, but does not know whether to be happy or sad. "I'm glad to be alive, but I feel a bit shaky."

Spotty grabs hold of Skeleton and flies back to the dome. The Spotty family is united and happy. Everyone is pleased that the cosmic dust has not fallen into evil hands. But where are Tex and Bulk?

Peering through a telescope, SuperTed spots them clinging to a branch over-hanging the ravine. Tex tries to kick off Bulk, who is hanging on to his trousers, a big enough problem to keep anyone quiet for a while.